Edwin Booth

Love and pride

Bulwer Lytton's drama of The lady of Lyons

Edwin Booth

Love and pride
Bulwer Lytton's drama of The lady of Lyons

ISBN/EAN: 9783337119065

Printed in Europe, USA, Canada, Australia, Japan

Cover: Foto ©Andreas Hilbeck / pixelio.de

More available books at **www.hansebooks.com**

DRAMA OF

THE LADY OF LYONS

OR

LOVE AND PRIDE

AS PRODUCED BY

EDWIN BOOTH.

Adapted from the Text of the Author's Edition, with Introductory Remarks, &c.,

By HENRY L. HINTON.

NEW YORK:

PUBLISHED BY HURD & HOUGHT[...]

INTRODUCTION.

THE *Lady of Lyons* was originally produced at Covent Garden Theater, London, in February, 1838, the manager, Mr. Macready, essaying the rôle of Claude Melnotte ; his performance of this character was always highly lauded by the critics. The first representation of the play in this country took place at the old Park Theater on the 14th of May, 1838. Mr. Ireland, in his *Records of the New York Stage,* speaks in high praise of the cast as a whole. Mr. Forrest took the part of Claude. Mr. Placide (Col. Damas), Mrs. Wheatley (Mme. Deschapelles), and Mrs. Richardson (Pauline), had parts peculiarly adapted to their several styles, and in which they have never been excelled, while Miss Cushman's talent raised a meager and insignificant character, Widow Melnotte, to an interesting and prominent position. The story upon which the play is founded, and the author's motive in presenting the piece, are given in his preface ; which is as follows :—

'An indistinct recollection of the very pretty little tale, called *The Bellows-Mender,* suggested the plot of this drama. The incidents are, however, greatly altered from those in the tale, and the characters entirely recast.

'Having long had a wish to illustrate certain periods of the French history, so, in the selection of the date in which the scenes of this play are laid, I saw that the era of the Republic was that in which the incidents were rendered most probable, in which the probationary career of the hero could well be made sufficiently rapid for dramatic effect, and in which the character of the time itself was depicted by the agencies necessary to the conduct of the narrative. For, during the early years of the first and most brilliant successes of the French Republic, in the general ferment of society, and the brief equalization of ranks, Claude's high-placed love, his ardent feelings, his unsettled principles (the struggle between which makes the passion of this drama), his ambition, and his career, were phenomena that characterized the age, and in which the spirit of the nation went along with the extravagance of the individual.

' The play itself was composed with a twofold object. In the first place, sympathizing with the enterprise of Mr. Macready, as manager of Covent Garden, and believing that many of the higher interests of the Drama were involved in the success or failure of an enterprise equally hazardous and disinterested, I felt, if I may so presume to express myself, something of the Brotherhood of Art; and it was only for Mr. Macready to think it possible that I might serve him, in order to induce me to make the attempt.

' Secondly, in that attempt I was mainly anxious to see whether or not, after the comparative failure on the stage of *The Duchess de la Vallière,* certain critics had truly declared that it was not in my power to attain the art of dramatic construction and theatrical effect. I felt, indeed, that it was in this that a writer, accustomed to the narrative class of composition, would have the most both to learn and *un*learn. Accordingly, it was to the development of the plot and the arrangement of the incidents that I directed my chief attention ; and I sought to throw whatever belongs to poetry less into the diction and the " felicity of words," than into the construction of the story, the creation of the characters, and the spirit of the pervading sentiment.

' The authorship of the play was neither avowed nor suspected until the play had established itself in public favor. The announcement of my name was the signal for attacks, chiefly political, to which it is now needless to refer. When a work has outlived for some time the earlier hostilities of criticism, there comes a new race of critics to which a writer may, for the most part, calmly trust for a fair consideration, whether of the faults or the merits of his performance.'

In adapting the present edition of this play to the stage, the editor has found it necessary to make but few variations from the original text. In truth few dramas, recent or old, have demanded so little pruning at the hands of stage-managers. The punctuation, however, has been modified, so as to make it accord with the system adopted in the other plays of this series.

COSTUME.

THE following remarks on the costume of the period of this play are translated from 'Herbe's Costumes Français':—

'The years '91 and '92, which were such sad ones for the Court, simplified the fashions of the time, without banishing elegance; but in '9. the fall of the throne, the invasion, the ruin of the finances, and the imperious demands of equality, brought all luxury under the ban; even the rich, reducing themselves to the level of people, pushed negligence of costume to the verge of indecency. The cargmagnole, or jacket, and the great-coat were generally worn; powdering and painting ceased to be practiced; and these tendencies in dress, together with the terrible events of the time, gave men a somber and fierce expression. Democracy having gone down with its leaders, the Thermidorians displayed an affectation of elegance; they resumed the custom of powdering; and, to give themselves an imposing air, they bound up, under the name of *oreilles de chien*, two masses of hair upon the cheeks, and allowed the rest to fall back in tresses. As a rallying signal, they put on very high green cravats. Frock and dress coats were very short and with wide lapels; breeches were worn with pumps and striped or spotted stockings, and tight pantaloons with top-boots. Toward '99, powdering was again discontinued, the *oreilles de chien* were suppressed, and the collars and lapels of coats lost somewhat of their width; but with the Consulate, the fashions of the court began to reappear—the nets or bags of hair, and powdered heads. Breeches, opera hats, and top-boots gave way, under the Empire, to tight pantaloons, black boots, and the round hat. In winter, cloaks were worn. In 1806 there arose a mania for wearing a round jacket over the dress-coat. Notwithstanding the proscription of powdered heads, despite the coiffures *à la Caracalla*, and those *à la Titus*, adopted by the Emperor, a multitude of people pertinaciously clung to their cues to the end of his reign.

'When the Republic was established, all thoughts were turned toward antiquity, to admire and copy the Greeks and Romans. Costumes, head-dresses, names, and house-furniture, all were fashioned after the antique. The ladies seized upon this novelty with eagerness, but the first attempts which they made after the Reign of Terror were original and barbarous. Like the men, they were powdered, and wore *oreilles de chien* and cravats; they dressed the head in the most bizarre styles; but the love of antiquity soon gave them a preference for the Greek and Roman head-dresses, and at the court of Barras, the ladies displayed, along with the most perfect taste, a forgetfulness of decency. To give the outline of the form was the dominant aim; thus, a caraco without sleeves, very short and low in the neck, a transparent robe with a long trail, a very fine and short petticoat, and flesh-colored stockings, formed the dress of a lady. Some strove to introduce the Roman mode, and donned the buskin, but without success. Under the Consulate, tunics were adopted, and the trails of the robes began to be curtailed till, at the commencement of the Empire, they were suppressed altogether. Finally, the mode lost all its elegance; the general attire became contracted and mean, and bad taste was carried so far as to make the skirts without folds. Under the Directory and the Consulate, the robes of ladies in full dress were so décolleté that the nipples of the breasts were revealed. Under the Empire much less of the bosom was displayed, but the robe was parted on the back down to the girdle. Very low coiffures and small hats were worn till 1811; then they kept increasing in size till the Restoration. In winter, shawls, furs, and tippets of swan's down, cashmeres, and short coats with many capes were adopted.

' Victorious over prejudices, reason became intolerant, and exiled religion. Then was born the dogma of the " Theophilantropes;" but this new religion, child of liberty, was doomed soon to perish with liberty itself. Its ministers were clothed in a long, white robe, gathered about the waist with a blue girdle with floating ends.

' Under the Directory, luxury reappeared in a garb of simplicity which accorded but little with modesty; for, although the ladies only clothed themselves in linen, they could not find textures fine enough, and there were shops where the threads were drawn out to render them more transparent and soft, so that, in all the movements and attitudes of the body, the dress revealed the shape in all its outlines. Flowers, diamonds, and especially cameos, composed the rest of the attire of ladies; and, although the men, under the Consulate, resumed gold and silver embroideries, ladies adorned their robes with them only at the imperial court Under the Directory, gold and silver were excluded from all the vestments of the civil authorities; but the tunic, the coat, and the cloak of the Directors were richly ornamented with them. The members of the *Chambre des Anciens* wore a violet robe, and a white mantle; the Cinq-Cents, a purple mantle and a white robe. The embroideries were tri-colored. The dress of the members of the High Court of Justice consisted of a robe, a white toga and mantle, bordered with red and blue cords; that of the members of the Tribunal of Appeal was composed of a blue toga and robe, white mantle, with tri-colored borders and red girdle. The members of the Civil and Criminal Tribunal, and the Justices of Peace, were arrayed in the same manner; the members of the Civil Tribunal were distinguished by a blue ribbon with a red and a white cord; those of the Criminal Tribunal, by a red ribbon with a white and a blue cord; Justices, by a white ribbon with a red and a blue cord, and a round hat without a plume. The President of the Municipal Administration appeared all in black, with a round hat decked with feathers and a tri-colored ribbon, and tri-colored scarf in form of a Saint Andrew's cross. The members of the Departmental Administration wore a black coat and black stockings, a tunic with blue linings and facings.

'The National Guard was created in 1789. Its uniform consisted of a blue coat, white vest, breeches, linings, gaiters, red facings, collar, epaulets, plume and bands, hat and bearskin caps.'

We have but little to add to this exhaustive account, and that is simply for the purpose of animadverting upon the practice of arraying Claude Melnotte in the garb of a prince. A moment's reflection will suffice to show the reader that, in the time of the play, an aristocratic costume would have brought our prince without delay to the guillotine. It is equally improper to array the peasant Melnotte in blouse and pantaloons instead of the true attire of the Lyonnese peasantry, which is described as follows:

'The dress in the district of the Leonais is, like its wearers, grave and formal; it is generally made of black cloth or serge, which gives it a most somber appearance. The coat is cut quite square, but sometimes reaches half way to the knee; at others, it is only like a long jacket. The waistcoat is very long. The breeches of the better farmers are very large, and tied at the knees; the poorer peasants have them not nearly so wide. The stockings are black, and a blue scarf encircles the waist; the hair always hangs at its full length over the back and shoulders; the hat is of immense size, and the shoe-buckle enormous. Those peasants who can not afford to wear cloth clothes have them made of linen, and wear straw hats, with black cotton rosette.'

DRAMATIS PERSONÆ

Of this adaptation of *The Lady of Lyons* as cast for its first representation at Booth's Theatre, New York,————————.

BEAUSEANT, in love with, and refused by, Pauline.........————————

GLAVIS, his friend, also a rejected suitor to Pauline.........————————

COLONEL DAMAS, cousin to Madame Deschappelles........———— ————

MONSIEUR DESCHAPPELLES, a Lyonese merchant, }
    father of Pauline......................... } ....————————

CLAUDE MELNOTTE, a gardener's son..................————————

GASPAR, his friend................................————— ————

First Officer ....———— A Landlord..............————————

Second Officer............———— A Servant................————————

Third Officer.............———— A Servant from the Inn.....————————

MADAME DESCHAPPELLES, wife to M. Deschappelles.......————————

PAULINE, her daughter.............................————————

WIDOW MELNOTTE, mother of Claude.................————————

JANET, daughter to the Landlord....................————————

MARIAN, maid to Pauline..........................————————

A Notary, Servants, &c.

SCENE: *Lyons, and the neighborhood.*

THE LADY OF LYONS;

OR,

LOVE AND PRIDE.

ACT I.

SCENE I. *A room in the house of M. Deschappelles at Lyons. The gardens are seen from the open window.*

PAULINE *reclining on a sofa,* MARIAN, *her Maid, fanning her. Flowers and notes on a table beside the sofa.* MADAME DES-CHAPPELLES *seated.*

Mme. D. Marian, put that rose a little more to the left. [*Marian alters the position of a rose in Pauline's hair.*] Ah, so! that improves the hair, the *tournure,* the *je ne sais quoi!* You are certainly very handsome, child! quite my style; I don't wonder that you make such a sensation! Old, young, rich, and poor, do homage to the Beauty of Lyons! Ah, we live again in our children, especially when they have our eyes and complexion!

Pau. [*Languidly*] Dear mother, you spoil your Pauline! [*Aside*] I wish I knew who sent me these flowers!

Mme. D. No, child! If I praise you, it is only to inspire you with a proper ambition. You are born to make a great marriage. Beauty is valuable or worthless according as you invest the property to the best advantage. Marian, go and order the carriage! [*Exit Marian.*

Pau. Who *can* it be that sends me, every day, these beautiful flowers? How sweet they are!

Enter SERVANT.

Ser. Monsieur Beauseant, madam.

Mme. D. Let him enter. [*Exit Servant.*] Pauline, this is another offer! I know it is! Your father should engage an additional clerk to keep the account-book of your conquests.

Enter BEAUSEANT.

Beau. Ah, ladies, how fortunate I am to find you at home! [*Aside*] How lovely she looks! It is a great sacrifice I make in marrying into a family in trade! they will be eternally grateful! [*Aloud*] Madam, you will permit me a word with your charming daughter. [*Approaches Pauline, who rises disdainfully.*] Mademoiselle, I have ventured to wait upon you, in a hope that you must long since have divined. Last night, when you outshone all the beauty of Lyons, you completed your conquest over me! You know that my fortune is not exceeded by any estate in the province; you know that, but for the Revolution, which has defrauded me of my titles, I should be noble. May I, then, trust that you will not reject my alliance? I offer you my hand and heart.

Pau. [*Aside*] He has the air of a man who confers a favour. [*Aloud*] Sir, you are very condescending, I thank you humbly; but being duly sensible of my own demerits, you must allow me to decline the honour you propose. [*Courtesies and turns away.*

Beau. Decline! impossible! you are not serious! Madam, suffer me to appeal to *you*. I am a suitor for your daughter's hand, the settlements shall be worthy her beauty and my station. May I wait on M. Deschappelles?

Mme. D. M. Deschappelles never interferes in the domestic arrangements. You are very obliging. If you were still a marquess, or if my daughter were intended to marry a commoner, why, perhaps we might give you the preference.

Beau. A commoner! we are all commoners in France now.

Mme. D. In France, yes; but there is a nobility still left in the other countries in Europe. We are quite aware of your good qualities, and don't doubt that you will find some lady more suitable to your pretensions. We shall be always happy to see you as an acquaintance, M. Beauseant! My dear child, the carriage will be here presently.

Beau. Say no more, madam! say no more! [*Aside*] Refused! and by a merchant's daughter! Refused! It will be all over Lyons before sunset! I will go and bury myself in my château, study philosophy, and turn woman-hater. Refused! they ought to be sent to a madhouse! Ladies, I have the honour to wish you a very good morning. [*Exit.*

Mme. D. How forward these men are! I think, child, we kept up our dignity. Any girl, however inexperienced, knows how to accept an offer, but it requires a vast deal of address to refuse one with proper condescension and disdain. I used to practice it at school with the dancing-master!

Enter DAMAS.

Dam. Good morning, cousin Deschappelles. Well, Pauline, you are recovered from last night's ball? So many triumphs must be very fatiguing. Even M. Glavis sighed most piteously when you departed; but that might be the effect of the supper.

Pau. M. Glavis, indeed!

Mme. D. M. Glavis! as if my daughter would think of M. Glavis!

Dam. Hey-dey! why not? His father left him a very pretty fortune, and his birth is higher than yours, cousin Deschappelles. But perhaps you are looking to M. Beauseant; his father was a marquess before the Revolution.

Pau. M. Beauseant! Cousin, you delight in tormenting me!

Mme. D. Don't mind him, Pauline! Cousin Damas, you have no susceptibility of feeling; there is a certain indelicacy in all your ideas. M. Beauseant knows already that he is no match for my daughter!

Dam. Pooh! pooh! one would think you intended your daughter to marry a prince!

Mme. D. Well, and if I did?—what then? Many a foreign prince—

Dam. [*Interrupting her*] Foreign prince! foreign fiddle-stick! you ought to be ashamed of such nonsense at your time of life.

Mme. D. My time of life! That is an expression never applied to any lady till she is sixty-nine and three-quarters; and only then by the clergyman of the parish.

Enter Servant.

Ser. Madam, the carriage is at the door.   [*Exit.*

Mme. D. Come, child, put on your bonnet; you really have a very thorough-bred air; not at all like your poor father. [*Fondly*] Ah, you little coquette! when a young lady is always making mischief, it is a sure sign that she takes after her mother!

Pau. Good day, cousin Damas, and a better humour to you. [*Going back to the table and taking the flowers*] Who *could* have sent me these flowers? [*Exeunt Pauline and Madame Deschappelles.*

Dam. That would be an excellent girl if her head had not been turned. I fear she is now become incorrigible! Zounds, what a lucky fellow I am to be still a bachelor! They may talk of the devotion of the sex, but the most faithful attachment in life is that of a woman in love—with herself.   [*Exit.*

Scene II. *The exterior of a small Village Inn, sign, the Golden Lion, a few leagues from Lyons.*

Beau. [*Behind the scenes*] Yes, you may bait the horses; we shall rest here an hour.

Enter Beauseant *and* Glavis.

Gla. Really, my dear Beauseant, consider that I have promised to spend a day or two with you at your château, that I am quite at your mercy for my entertainment, and yet you are as silent and gloomy as a mute at a funeral, or an Englishman at a party of pleasure.

Beau. Bear with me! the fact is that I am miserable!

Gla. You, the richest and gayest bachelor in Lyons?

Beau. It is because I am a bachelor that I am miserable. Thou knowest Pauline, the only daughter of the rich merchant, M. Deschappelles?

Gla. Know her? who does not? As pretty as Venus and as proud as Juno.

Beau. Her taste is worse than her pride. [*Drawing himself up*] Know, Glavis, she has actually refused *me!*

Gla. [*Aside*] So she has me! very consoling! In all cases of heart-ache, the application of another man's disappointment draws out the pain, and allays the irritation. [*Aloud*] Refused you! and wherefore?

Beau. I know not, unless it be because the Revolution swept away my father's title of marquess, and she will not marry a commoner. Now, as we have no noblemen left in France, as we are all citizens and equals, she can only hope that, in spite of the war, some English Milord or German Count will risk his life by coming to Lyons, that this *fille du Roturier* may condescend to accept him. Refused me, and with scorn! By heaven, I'll not submit to it tamely: I'm in a perfect fever of mortification and rage. Refused *me*, indeed!

Gla. Be comforted, my dear fellow, I will tell you a secret. For the same reason she refused *me!*

Beau. You! that's a very different matter! But give me your hand, Glavis, we'll think of some plan to humble her. *Mille diables!* I should like to see her married to a strolling player!

Enter Landlord *from the Inn.*

Land. Your servant, citizen Beauseant, servant, sir. Perhaps you will take dinner before you proceed to your château; our larder is most plentifully supplied.

Beau. I have no appetite.

Gla. Nor I. Still it is bad travelling on an empty stomach. What have you got? [*Takes and looks over bill of fare.*

[*Shout within*: 'Long live the Prince! Long live the Prince!'

Beau. The prince! what prince is that? I thought we had no princes left in France.

Land. Ha! ha! the lads always call him prince. He has just won the prize in a shooting-match, and they are taking him home in triumph.

Beau. Him! and who's Mr. Him?

Land. Who should he be but the pride of the village, Claude Melnotte? Of course you have heard of Claude Melnotte.

Gla. [*Giving back the bill of fare*] Never had that honour. Soup, ragout of hare, roast chicken, and, in short, all you have!

Beau. The son of old Melnotte, the gardener?

Land. Exactly so, a wonderful young man.

Beau. How, wonderful? Are his cabbages better than other people's?

Land. Nay, he don't garden any more; his father left him well off. He's only a genus.

Gla. A what?

Land. A genus! a man who can do everything in life except anything that's useful; that's a genus.

Beau. You raise my curiosity; proceed.

Land. Well, then, about four years ago, old Melnotte died, and left his son well to do in the world. We then all observed that a great change came over young Claude: he took to reading and Latin, and hired a professor from Lyons, who had so much in his head that he was forced to wear a great full-bottom wig to cover it. Then he took a fencing-master, and a dancing-master, and a music-master; and then he learned to paint; and at last it was said that young Claude was to go to Paris, and set up for a painter. The lads laughed at him at first; but he is a stout fellow, is Claude, and as brave as a lion, and soon taught them to laugh the wrong side of their mouths; and now all the boys swear by him, and all the girls pray for him.

Beau. A promising youth, certainly! And why do they call him prince?

Land. Partly because he is at the head of them all, and partly because he has such a proud way with him, and wears such fine clothes, and in short, looks like a prince.

Beau. And what could have turned the foolish fellow's brain? The Revolution, I suppose?

Land. Yes, the revolution that turns us all topsy-turvy, the revolution of Love.

Beau. Romantic young Corydon. And with whom is he in love?

Land. Why, but it is a secret, gentlemen.

Beau. Oh! certainly.

Land. Why, then, I hear from his mother, good soul! that it is no less a person than the Beauty of Lyons, Pauline Deschappelles.

Beau. and Gla. Ha! ha! Capital!

Land. You may laugh, but it is as true as I stand here.

Beau. And what does the Beauty of Lyons say to his suit?

Land. Lord, sir, she never even condescended to look at him, though when he was a boy he worked in her father's garden.

Beau. Are you sure of that?

Land. His mother says that Mademoiselle does not know him by sight.

Beau. [*Taking Glavis aside*] I have hit it, I have hit it; here is our revenge! Here is a prince for our haughty damsel. Do you take me?

Gla. Deuce take me if I do!

Beau. Blockhead! it's as clear as a map. What if we could make this elegant clown pass himself off as a foreign prince? lend him money, clothes, equipages for the purpose? make him propose to Pauline? marry Pauline? Would it not be delicious?

Gla. Ha! ha! Excellent! But how shall we support the necessary expenses of his highness?

Beau. Pshaw! Revenge is worth a much larger sacrifice than

a few hundred louis ; as for details, my valet is the truest fellow
in the world, and shall have the appointment of his highness'
establishment.   Let's go to him at once, and see if he be really
this Admirable Crichton.

Gla. With all my heart ; but the dinner ?

Beau. Always thinking of dinner !   Hark ye, landlord ; how
far is it to young Melnotte's cottage ?   I should like to see such
a prodigy.

Land. Turn down the lane, then strike across the common,
and you will see his mother's cottage.

Beau. True, he lives with his mother.   [*Aside*] We will not
trust to an old woman's discretion ; better send for him hither !
I'll just step in and write him a note.   Come, Glavis.

Gla. Yes, Beauseant, Glavis and Co., manufacturers of princes,
wholesale and retail,—an uncommonly genteel line of business.
But why so grave ?

Beau. You think only of the sport, I of the revenge.

[*Exeunt within the Inn.*

Scene III.   *The interior of Melnotte's Cottage.*

*Flowers placed here and there; a guitar on an oaken table, with
a portfolio, &c.; a picture on an easel, covered by a curtain,
fencing-foils crossed over the mantel-piece, an attempt at refinement in spite of the homeliness of the furniture, &c., a staircase to the right conducts to the upper story.*

Widow Melnotte *discovered.*

[*Shout within :* ' Long live Claude Melnotte !   Long live the
Prince !']

Wid. Hark ! there's my dear son ; carried off the prize, I'm
sure ; and now he'll want to treat them all.

Claude Melnotte. [*Opening the door*] What ! you will not come
in, my friends !   Well, well, there's a trifle to make merry else-
where.   Good day to you all, good day !

[*Shouts within :*   ' Hurrah ! Long live Prince Claude !'

Enter CLAUDE MELNOTTE, *with a rifle in his hand.*

Mel. Give me joy, dear mother! I've won the prize! never missed one shot! Is it not handsome, this gun?

Wid. Humph! Well, what is it worth, Claude?

Mel. Worth! What is a riband worth to a soldier? Worth! everything! Glory is priceless!

Wid. Leave glory to great folks. Ah! Claude, Claude! castles in the air cost a vast deal to keep up! How is all this to end? What good does it do thee to learn Latin, and sing songs, and play on the guitar, and fence, and dance, and paint pictures? All very fine; but what does it bring in?

Mel. Wealth! wealth, my mother! Wealth to the mind, wealth to the heart, high thoughts, bright dreams, the hope of fame, the ambition to be worthier to love Pauline.

Wid. My poor son! The young lady will never think of thee.

Mel. Do the stars think of us? Yet if the prisoner see them shine in his dungeon, wouldst thou bid him turn away from *their* lustre? Even from this low cell, poverty, I lift my eyes to Pauline and forget my chains. [*Goes to the picture and draws aside the curtain*] See, this is her image, painted from memory. Oh, how the canvas wrongs her! [*Takes up the brush and throws it aside*] I shall never be a painter! I can paint no likeness but one, and that is above all art. I would turn soldier, France needs soldiers! But to leave the air that Pauline breathes! What is the hour? so late? I will tell thee a secret, mother. Thou knowest that for the last six weeks I have sent every day the rarest flowers to Pauline? she wears them. I have seen them on her breast. Ah, and then the whole universe seemed filled with odours! I have now grown more bold, I have poured my worship into poetry, I have sent verses to Pauline, I have signed them with my own name. My messenger ought to be back by this time. I bade him wait for an answer.

Wid. And what answer do you expect, Claude?

Mel. That which the Queen of Navarre sent to the poor

troubadour: 'Let me see the Oracle that can tell nations I am beautiful!' She will admit me. I shall hear her speak, I shall meet her eyes, I shall read upon her cheek the sweet thoughts that translate themselves into blushes. Then, then, oh, then, she may forget that I am the peasant's son!

Wid. Nay, if she will but hear thee talk, Claude!

Mel. I foresee it all. She will tell me that desert is the true rank. She will give me a badge, a flower, a glove! Oh, rapture! I shall join the armies of the Republic, I shall rise, I shall win a name that beauty will not blush to hear. I shall return with the right to say to her, 'See, how love does not level the proud, but raise the humble!' Oh, how my heart swells within me! Oh, what glorious prophets of the future are youth and hope! [*Knock at the door.*

Wid. Come in.

Enter GASPAR.

Mel. Welcome, Gaspar, welcome. Where is the letter? Why do you turn away, man? where is the letter? [*Gaspar gives him one*] This! This is mine, the one I entrusted to thee. Didst thou not leave it?

Gas. Yes, I left it.

Mel. My own verses returned to me! Nothing else?

Gas. Thou wilt be proud to hear how thy messenger was honoured. For thy sake, Melnotte, I have borne that which no Frenchman can bear without disgrace.

Mel. Disgrace, Gaspar! Disgrace?

Gas. I gave thy letter to the porter, who passed it from lackey to lackey till it reached the lady it was meant for.

Mel. It reached her, then; you are sure of that? It reached her; well, well!

Gas. It reached her, and was returned to me with blows. Dost hear, Melnotte? with blows! Death! are we slaves still, that we are to be thus dealt with, we peasants?

Mel. With blows? No, Gaspar, no; not blows!

Gas. I could show thee the marks if it were not so deep a

shame to bear them. The lackey who tossed thy letter into the mire swore that his lady and her mother never were so insulted. What could thy letter contain, Claude?

Mel. [*Looking over the letter*] Not a line that a serf might not have written to an empress. No, not one.

Gas. They promise thee the same greeting they gave me, if thou wilt pass that way. Shall we endure this, Claude?

Mel. [*Wringing Gaspar's hand*] Forgive me, the fault was mine, I have brought this on thee; I will not forget it; thou shalt be avenged! The heartless insolence!

Gas. Thou art moved, Melnotte; think not of me; I would go through fire and water to serve thee; but a blow! It is not the *bruise* that galls, it is the *blush*, Melnotte!

Mel. Say, what message? How insulted! Wherefore? What the offence?

Gas. Did you not write to Pauline Deschappelles, the daughter of the rich merchant?

Mel. Well?

Gas. Are you not a peasant, a gardener's son? that was the offence. Sleep on it, Melnotte. Blows to a French citizen, blows! [*Exit.*

Wid. Now you are cured, Claude!

Mel. [*Tearing the letter*] So do I scatter her image to the winds; I will stop her in the open streets, I will insult her, I will beat her menial ruffians, I will—[*Turns suddenly to Widow*] Mother, am I hump-backed, deformed, hideous?

Wid. You!

Mel. A coward, a thief, a liar?

Wid. You!

Mel. Or a dull fool, a vain, drivelling, brainless idiot?

Wid. No, no.

Mel. What am I then, worse than all these? Why, I am a peasant! What has a peasant to do with love? Vain Revolutions, why lavish your cruelty on the great? Oh, that we, we, the hewers of wood and drawers of water, had been swept away, so that the proud might learn what the world would be without us.   [*Knock at the door.*

Enter Servant *from the Inn.*

Ser. A letter for Citizen Melnotte.

Mel. A letter! from her perhaps; who sent thee?

Ser. Why, Monsieur, I mean Citizen, Beauseant, who stops to dine at the Golden Lion, on his way to his château.

Mel. Beauseant! [*Reads.*] 'Young man, I know thy secret, thou lovest above thy station: if thou hast wit, courage, and discretion, I can secure to thee the realization of thy most sanguine hopes; and the sole condition I ask in return is, that thou shalt be steadfast to thine own ends. I shall demand from thee a solemn oath to marry her whom thou lovest; to bear her to thine home on thy wedding night. I am serious; if thou wouldst learn more, lose not a moment, but follow the bearer of this letter to thy friend and patron—CHARLES BEAUSEANT.'

Mel. Can I believe my eyes? Are our own passions the sorcerers that raise up for us spirits of good or evil? I will go instantly.   [*Exit Servant.*

Wid. What is this, Claude!

Mel. 'Marry her whom thou lovest'—'bear her to thine own home.' Oh, revenge and love; which of you is the stronger? [*Gazing on the picture*] Sweet face, thou smilest on me from the canvas: weak fool that I am, do I then love her still? No, it is the vision of my own romance that I have worshipped: it is the reality to which I bring scorn for scorn. Adieu, mother: I will return anon. · My brain reels, the earth swims before me. [*Looking again at the letter*] No, it is *not* a mockery; I do not dream!   *Exit.—The curtain falls.*

ACT II.

SCENE I. *The gardens of M. Deschappelles' house at Lyons. The house seen at the back of the stage.*

Enter BEAUSEANT *and* GLAVIS.

Beau. Well, what think you of my plot? Has it not succeeded to a miracle? The instant that I introduced his highness the Prince of Como, to the pompous mother and the scornful daughter, it was all over with them: he came, he saw, he conquered: and, though it is not many days since he arrived, they have already promised him the hand of Pauline.

Gla. It is lucky, though, that you told them his highness travelled incognito, for fear the Directory—who are not very fond of princes—should lay him by the heels; for he has a wonderful wish to keep up his rank, and scatters our gold about with as much coolness as if he were watering his own flower-pots.

Beau. True, he is damnably extravagant; I think the sly dog does it out of malice. However, it must be owned that he reflects credit on his loyal subjects, and makes a very pretty figure in his fine clothes with my diamond snuff-box.

Gla. And my diamond ring! But do you think that he will be firm to the last? I fancy I see symptoms of relenting: he will never keep up his rank, if he once let out his conscience.

Beau. His oath binds him; he cannot retract without being forsworn, and those low fellows are always superstitious! But as it is, I tremble lest he be discovered: that bluff Colonel Damas—Madame Deschappelles' cousin—evidently suspects him: we must make haste and conclude the farce: I have thought of a plan to end it this very day.

Gla. This very day! Poor Pauline! her dream will be soon over.

Beau. Yes, this day they shall be married; this evening, according to his oath, he shall carry his bride to the Golden Lion, and then pomp, equipage, retinue, and title, all shall vanish at once; and her highness, the princess, shall find that she has refused the son of a marquess, to marry the son of a gardener. Oh, Pauline! once loved, now hated, yet still not relinquished, thou shalt drain the cup to the dregs, thou shalt know what it is to be humbled!

Enter, from the house, MELNOTTE, *as the Prince of Como, leading in* PAULINE; MADAME DESCHAPPELLES *fanning herself, and* COLONEL DAMAS.

> [*Beauseant and Glavis bow respectfully. Pauline and Melnotte walk apart.*

Mme. D. Good morning, gentlemen; really I am so fatigued with laughter; the dear prince is so entertaining. What wit he has! Any one might see that he has spent his whole life in courts.

Dam. And what the deuce do you know about courts, cousin Deschappelles? You women regard men just as you buy books; you never care about what is in them, but how they are bound and lettered. 'Sdeath, I don't think you would even look at your Bible, if it had not a title to it.

Mme. D. How coarse you are, cousin Damas! quite the manners of a barrack; you don't deserve to be one of our family; really we must drop your acquaintance when Pauline marries. I cannot patronize any relations that would discredit my future son-in-law, the Prince of Como.

Mel. [*Advancing*] These are beautiful gardens, madam. [*Beauseant and Glavis retire.*] Who planned them?

Mme. D. A gardener named Melnotte, your highness, an honest man who knew his station. I can't say as much for his son, a presuming fellow, who, ha! ha! actually wrote verses, such doggerel! to my daughter.

Pau. Yes, how you would have laughed at them, Prince! *you* who write such beautiful verses!

Mel. This Melnotte must be a monstrous impudent person!

Dam. Is he good-looking ?

Mme. D. I never notice such *canaille ;* an ugly, mean-looking clown, if I remember right.

Dam. Yet I heard your porter say he was wonderfully like his highness.

Mel. [*Taking snuff*] You are complimentary.

Mme. D. For shame, cousin Damas ! like the prince, indeed.

Pau. Like you ! Ah, mother, like our beautiful prince ! I'll never speak to you again, cousin Damas.

Mel. [*Aside*] Hum ! rank is a great beautifier ! I never passed for an Apollo while I was a peasant ; if I am so handsome as a prince, what should I be as an emperor ? [*Aloud*] Monsieur Beauseant, will you honour me ? [*Offers snuff.*

Beau. No, your highness ; I have no small vices.

Mel. Nay, if it were a vice, you'd be sure to have it, Monsieur Beauseant.

Mme. D. Ha ! ha ! how very severe ! what wit !

Beau. [*In a rage and aside*] Curse his impertinence !

Mme. D. What a superb snuff-box !

Pau. And what a beautiful ring !

Mel. You like the box, a trifle, interesting perhaps from associations, a present from Louis XIV. to my great-great-grand-mother. Honour me by accepting it.

Beau. [*Plucking him by the sleeve*] How ! what the devil ! My box ! are you mad ! It is worth five hundred louis.

Mel. [*Unheeding him and turning to Pauline*] And you like this ring ? Ah, it has indeed a lustre since your eyes have shone on it. [*Placing it on her finger*] Henceforth hold me, sweet enchantress, the Slave of the Ring.

Gla. [*Pulling him*] Stay, stay, what are you about ? My maiden aunt's legacy, a diamond of the first water. You shall be hanged for swindling, sir.

Mel. [*Pretending not to hear*] It is curious, this ring ; it is the one with which my grandfather, the Doge of Venice, married the Adriatic ! [*Madame and Pauline examine the ring.*

Mel. [*To Beauseant and Glavis*] Fie, gentlemen! princes must be generous! [*Turns to Damas, who watches them closely*] These kind friends have my interest so much at heart, that they are as careful of my property as if it were their own.

Beau. and Gla. [*Confusedly*] Ha! ha! very good joke that!

[*Appear to remonstrate with Melnotte in dumb show.*

Dam. What's all that whispering? I am sure there is some juggle here: hang me, if I think he is an Italian after all. 'Gad! I'll try him. Servitore umillissimo, Excellenza.[1]

Mel. Hum, what does he mean, I wonder?

Dam. Godo di vedervi in buona salute.[2]

Mel. Hem, hem!

Dam. Fa bel tempo! che si dice di nuovo?[3]

Mel. Well, sir, what's all that gibberish?

Dam. Oh, oh! only Italian, your highness! The Prince of Como does not understand his own language!

Mel. Not as you pronounce it; who the deuce could?

Mme. D. Ha! ha! cousin Damas, never pretend to what you don't know.

Pau. Ha! ha! cousin Damas; *you* speak Italian, indeed!

[*Makes a mocking gesture at him.*

Beau. [*To Glavis*] Clever dog! how ready!

Gla. Ready, yes; with my diamond ring! Damn his readiness!

Dam. Laugh at me! laugh at a colonel in the French army! The fellow's an impostor; I know he is. I'll see if he understands fighting as well as he does Italian. [*Goes up to him and, aside*] Sir, you are a jackanapes! Can you construe that?

Mel. No, sir; I never construe affronts in the presence of ladies; by-and-by I shall be happy to take a lesson, or give one.

Dam. I'll find the occasion, never fear!

Mme. D. Where are you going, cousin?

[1] Your Excellency's most humble servant.   [2] I am glad to see you in good health.
[3] Fine weather! what news is there?

Dam. To correct my Italian.   [*Exit.*

Beau. [*To Glavis*] Let us after and pacify him ; he evidently suspects something.

Gla. Yes! but my diamond ring!

Beau. And my box! We are over-taxed, fellow-subject! we must stop the supplies, and dethrone the prince.

Gla. Prince! he ought to be heir-apparent to King Stork!

[*Exeunt Beauseant and Glavis.*

Mme. D. Dare I ask your highness to forgive my cousin's insufferable vulgarity?

Pau. Oh yes! you will forgive his manner for the sake of his heart.

Mel. And the sake of his cousin. Ah, madam, there is one comfort in rank, we are so sure of our position that we are not easily affronted. Besides, M. Damas has bought the right of indulgence from his friends, by never showing it to his enemies.

Pau. Ah! he is, indeed, as brave in action as he is rude in speech. He rose from the ranks to his present grade, and in two years.

Mel. In two years! two years, did you say?

Mme. D. [*Aside*] I don't like leaving girls alone with their lovers ; but with a prince, it would be so ill-bred to be prudish!

[*Exit.*

Mel. You can be proud of your connection with one who owes his position to merit, not birth.

Pau. Why, yes ; but still—

Mel. Still what, Pauline?

Pau. There is something glorious in the heritage of command. A man who has ancestors is like a representative of the past.

Mel. True ; but, like other representatives, nine times out of ten he is a silent member. Ah, Pauline! not to the past, but to the future, looks true nobility, and finds its blazon in posterity.

Pau. You say this to please me, who have no ancestors ; but you, prince, must be proud of so illustrious a race!

Mel. No, no! I would not, were I fifty times a prince, be a pensioner on the dead! I honour birth and ancestry, when they are regarded as the incentives to exertion, not the title-deeds to sloth! I honour the laurels that overshadow the graves of our fathers; it is our 'fathers I emulate, when I desire that beneath the evergreen I myself have planted, my own ashes may repose! Dearest! couldst thou but see with my eyes!

Pau. I cannot forego pride when I look on thee, and think that thou lovest me. Sweet prince, tell me again of thy palace by the Lake of Como; it is so pleasant to hear of thy splendours, since thou didst swear to me that they would be desolate without Pauline; and when thou describest them, it is with a mocking lip and a noble scorn, as if custom had made thee disdain greatness.

Mel. Nay, dearest, nay, if thou wouldst have me paint
The home to which, could love fulfil its prayers,
This hand would lead thee, listen![1]   A deep vale
Shut out by Alpine hills from the rude world ;
Near a clear lake, margin'd by fruits of gold
And whispering myrtles ; glassing softest skies,
As cloudless, save with rare and roseate shadows,
As I would have thy fate !

Pau.   My own dear love !

Mel. A palace lifting to eternal summer
Its marble walls, from out a glossy bower
Of coolest foliage musical with birds,
Whose songs should syllable thy name !   At noon
We'd sit beneath the arching vines, and wonder
Why Earth could be unhappy, while the Heavens
Still left us youth and love !   We'd have no friends

---

[1] The reader will observe that Melnotte evades the request of Pauline. He proceeds to describe a home, which he does not say he possesses, but to which he would lead her, '*could Love fulfil its prayers.*' This caution is intended as a reply to a sagacious critic who censures the description, because it is not an exact and prosaic inventory of the characteristics of the Lake of Como! When Melnotte, for instance, talks of birds 'that syllable the name of Pauline,'—by the way, a literal translation from an Italian poet— he is not thinking of ornithology, but probably of the Arabian Nights. He is venting the extravagant, but natural, enthusiasm of the poet and the lover.

That were not lovers ; no ambition, save
To excel them all in love ; we'd read no books
That were not tales of love, that we might smile
To think how poorly eloquence of words
Translates the poetry of hearts like ours !
And when night came, amidst the breathless Heavens
We'd guess what star should be our home when love
Becomes immortal ; while the perfumed light
Stole through the mists of alabaster lamps,
And every air was heavy with the sighs
Of orange-groves and music from sweet lutes,
And murmurs of low fountains that gush forth
I' the midst of roses ! Dost thou like the picture ?

Pau. Oh, as the bee upon the flower, I hang
Upon the honey of thy eloquent tongue !
Am I not blest ?   And if I love too wildly,
Who would not love thee, like Pauline ?

Mel.   [*Bitterly*] Oh, false one !
It is the *prince* thou lovest, not the *man ;*
If in the stead of luxury, pomp, and power,
I had painted poverty, and toil, and care,
Thou hadst found no honey on my tongue ; Pauline,
That is not love !

Pau.   ·   Thou wrong'st me, cruel prince !
At first, in truth, I might not have been won,
Save through the weakness of a flatter'd pride ;
But *now*, oh ! trust me ; couldst thou fall from power
And sink—

Mel.   As low as that poor gardener's son
Who dared to lift his eyes to thee ?—

Pau.   Even then,
Methinks thou wouldst be only made more dear
By the sweet thought that I could prove how deep
Is woman's love ! We are like the insects, caught
By the poor glittering of a garish flame ;

But oh, the wings once scorch'd, the brightest star
Lures us no more ; and by the fatal light
We cling till death !

Mel.   Angel ! [*Aside*] Oh conscience ! conscience !
It must not be ; her love hath grown a torture
Worse than her hate. I will at once to Beauseant,
And—ha ! he comes. Sweet love, one moment leave me.
I have business with these gentlemen—I—I
Will forthwith join you.

Pau.   Do not tarry long !   [*Exit.*

Enter BEAUSEANT *and* GLAVIS.

Mel. Release me from my oath. I will not marry her !

Beau. Then thou art perjured.

Mel. No, I was not in my senses when I swore to thee to
marry her ! I was blind to all but her scorn ! deaf to all but my
passion and my rage ! Give me back my poverty and my honour !

Beau. It is too late, you must marry her ! and this day ! I
have a story already coined, and sure to pass current. This
Damas suspects thee, he will set the police to work ; thou wilt be
detected, Pauline will despise and execrate thee. Thou wilt be
sent to the common gaol as a swindler.

Mel. Fiend !

Beau. And in the heat of the girl's resentment—you know of
what resentment is capable—and the parents' shame, she will be
induced to marry the first that offers, even perhaps your humble
servant.

Mel. You ! No ; that were worse, for thou hast no mercy !
I will marry her, I will keep my oath. Quick, then, with the
damnable invention thou art hatching ; quick, if thou wouldst
not have me strangle thee or myself.

Gla. What a tiger ! Too fierce for a prince ; he ought to have
been the Grand Turk.

Beau. Enough, I will despatch ; be prepared.
            [*Exeunt Beauseant and Glavis.*

Dam. Now, then, sir, the ladies are no longer your excuse. I have brought you a couple of dictionaries; let us see if your highness can find out the Latin for *bilbo*.

Mel. Away, sir! I am in no humour for jesting.

Dam. I see you understand something of the grammar; you decline the noun-substantive 'small-sword' with great ease; but that won't do, you must take a lesson in *parsing*.

Mel. Fool!

Dam. Sir, as sons take after their mother, so the man who calls me a fool insults the lady who bore me; there's no escape for you, fight you shall, or—

Mel. Oh, enough, enough! take your ground. [*They fight, Damas is disarmed. Melnotte takes up the sword and returns it to Damas respectfully.*] A just punishment to the brave soldier who robs the state of its best property—the sole right to his valour and his life!

Dam. Sir, you fence exceedingly well; you must be a man of honour; I don't care a jot whether you are a prince; but a man who has carte and tierce at his fingers' ends must be a gentleman.

Mel. [*Aside*] Gentleman! Ay, I was a gentleman before I turned conspirator; for honest men are the gentlemen of Nature! Colonel, they tell me you rose from the ranks

Dam. I did.

Mel. And in two years?

Dam. It is true; that's no wonder in our army at present. Why, the oldest general in the service is scarcely thirty, and we have some of two-and-twenty.

Mel. Two-and-twenty!

Dam. Yes; in the French army, now-a-days, promotion is not a matter of purchase. We are all heroes, because we may be all generals. We have no fear of the cypress, because we may all hope for the laurel.

Mel. A general at two-and-twenty ! [*Turning away*] Sir, I may ask of you a favour one of these days.

Dam. Sir, I shall be proud to grant it. It is astonishing how much I like a man after I've fought with him !

[*Hides the swords.*

Enter MADAME DESCHAPPELLES *and* BEAUSEANT.

Mme. D. Oh, prince, prince ! What do I hear ? You must fly, you must quit us !

Mel. I !

Beau. Yes, prince : read this letter, just received from my friend at Paris, one of the Directory ; they suspect you of designs against the Republic : they are very suspicious of princes, and your family take part with the Austrians. Knowing that I introduced your highness at Lyons, my friend writes to me to say that you must quit the town immediately, or you will be arrested, thrown into prison, perhaps guillotined ! Fly ! I will order horses to your carriage instantly. Fly to Marseilles ; there you can take ship to Leghorn.

Mme. D. And what's to become of Pauline ? Am I not to be a mother to a princess, after all ?

Enter PAULINE *and* MONSIEUR DESCHAPPELLES.

Pau. [*Throwing herself into Melnotte's arms*] You must leave us ! Leave Pauline !

Beau. Not a moment is to be wasted.

M. Des. I will go to the magistrates and inquire—

Beau. Then he is lost ; the magistrates, hearing he is suspected, will order his arrest.

Mme. D. And shall I not be Princess Dowager ?

Beau. Why not ? There is only one thing to be done : send for the priest, let the marriage take place at once, and the prince carry home a bride !

Mel. Impossible ! [*Aside*] Villain !

Mme. D. What, lose my child ?

Beau. And gain a princess !

Mme. D. Oh, Monsieur Beauseant, you are so very kind, it must be so, we ought not to be selfish, my daughter's happiness is at stake. She will go away, too, in a carriage and six!

Pau. Thou art here still; I cannot part from thee, my heart will break.

Mel. But thou wilt not consent to this hasty union? thou wilt not wed an outcast, a fugitive?

Pau. Ah! If thou art in danger, who should share it but Pauline?

Mel. [*Aside*] Distraction! If the earth could swallow me!

M. Des. Gently! gently! The settlements, the contracts, my daughter's dowry!

Mel. The dowry! I am not base enough for that; no, not one farthing!

Beau. [*To Madame*] Noble fellow! Really, your good husband is too mercantile in these matters. Monsieur Deschappelles, you hear his highness: we can arrange the settlements by proxy; 'tis the way with people of quality.

M. Des. But—

Mme. D. Hold your tongue! Don't expose yourself!

Beau. I will bring the priest in a trice. Go in all of you and prepare; the carriage shall be at the door before the ceremony is over.

Mme. D. Be sure there are six horses, Beauseant! You are very good to have forgiven us for refusing you; but, you see—a prince!

Beau. And such a prince! Madam, I cannot blush at the success of so illustrious a rival. [*Aside*] Now will I follow them to the village, enjoy my triumph, and to-morrow, in the hour of thy shame and grief, I think, proud girl, thou wilt prefer even these arms to those of the gardener's son.   [*Exit.*

Mme D. Come, Monsieur Deschappelles, give your arm to her highness that is to be.

M. Des. I don't like doing business in such a hurry; 'tis not the way with the house of Deschappelles and Co.

Mme. D. There, now, you fancy you are in the counting-house, don't you ?   [*Pushes him to Pauline.*

Mel. Stay, stay, Pauline, one word. Have you no scruple, no fear ? Speak, it is not yet too late. —

Pau. When I loved thee, thy fate became mine. Triumph or danger, joy or sorrow, I am by thy side.

Dam. Well, well, prince, thou art a lucky man to be so loved. She is a good little girl in spite of her foibles ; make her as happy as if she were not to be a princess. [*Slapping him on the shoulder*] Come, . sir, I wish you joy, young, tender, lovely ; zounds, I envy you !

Mel. [*Who has stood apart in gloomy abstraction.*]
Do you ?   Wise judges are we of each other.
You envy me ! I thank you ! You may read
My joy upon my brow.   I thank you, sir !
If hearts had audible language, you would hear
What mine would answer when you talk of *envy.*

[*The curtain falls.*

ACT III.

SCENE I.   *The exterior of the Golden Lion ; time, twilight. The moon rises during the scene.*

Enter Landlord *and his* Daughter *from the Inn.*

Land. Ha ! ha ! ha ! Well, I never shall get over it. Our Claude is a prince with a vengeance now. His carriage breaks down at my inn ; ha ! ha !

Janet. And what airs the young lady gives herself ! ‘ Is this the best room you have, young woman ?’ with such a toss of the head !

Land. Well, get in, Janet, get in and see to the supper : the servants must sup before they go back.   [*Exeunt.*

Enter BEAUSEANT *and* GLAVIS.

Beau. You see our princess is lodged at last ; one stage more, and she'll be at her journey's end, the beautiful palace at the foot of the Alps ! ha ! ha !

Gla. Faith, I pity the poor Pauline, especially if she's going to sup at the Goldèn Lion. [*Makes a wry face.*] I shall never forget that cursed ragout.

Enter MELNOTTE *from the Inn.*

Beau. Your servant, my prince ; you reigned most worthily. I condole with you on your abdication. I am afraid that your highness' retinue are not very faithful servants. I think they will quit you in the moment of your fall, 'tis the fate of greatness. But you are welcome to your fine clothes, also the diamond snuff-box, which Louis XIV. gave to your great-great-grandmother.

Gla. And the ring, with which your grandfathèr the Doge of Venice married the Adriatic.

Mel. I have kept my oath, gentlemen ; say, have I kept my oath ?

Beau. Most religiously.

Mel. Then you have donè with me and mine, away with you !

Beau. How, knave ?

Mel. Look you, our bond is over. Proud conquerors that we are, we have won the victory over a simple girl, compromised her honour, embittered her life, blasted, in their very blossoms, all the flowers of her youth. This is your triumph ; it is my shame ! [*Turns to Beauseant*] Enjoy that triumph, but not in my sight. I *was* her betrayer, I *am* her protéctor ! Cross but her path, one word of scorn, one look of insult, nay, but one quiver of that mocking lip, and I will teach thee that bitter word ·thou hast graven eternally in this heart— *Repentance !*

Beau. His highness is most grandiloquent.

Mel. Highness me no more ! Beware ! Remorse has made me a new being. Away with you ! There is danger in me. Away !

Gla. [*Aside*] He's an awkward fellow to deal with : come away, Beauseant.

·*Beau.* I know the respéct due to rank. Adieu, my prince.

2*

Any commands at Lyons ? Yet hold, I promised you two hundred louis on your wedding-day ; here they are.

Mel. [*Dashing the purse to the ground*] I gave you revenge, I did not sell it. Take up your silver, Judas ; take it. Ay, it is fit you should learn to stoop.

Beau. You will beg my pardon for this some day. [*Aside to Glavis*] Come to my château, I shall return hither to-morrow to learn how Pauline likes her new dignity.

Mel. Are you not gone yet ?

Beau. Your highness' most obedient, most faithful—

Gla. And most humble servants. Ha ! ha !

[*Exeunt Beauseant and Glavis.*

Mel. Thank heaven I had no weapon, or I should have slain them. Wretch ! what can I say ? where turn ? On all sides mockery ; the very boors within—[*Laughter from the Inn*] 'Sdeath, if even in this short absence the exposure should have chanced. I will call her. We will go hence. I have already sent one I can trust to my mother's house. There, at least, none can insult her agony, gloat upon her shame ! There alone must she learn what a villain she has sworn to love. [*As he turns to the door—*

Enter PAULINE *from the Inn.*

Pau. Ah ! my lord, what a place ! I never saw such rude people. They stare and wink so. I think the very sight of a prince, though he travels *incognito*, turns their honest heads. What a pity the carriage should break down in such a spot ! You are not well, the drops stand on your brow, your hand is feverish.

Mel. Nay, it is but a passing spasm ; the air—

Pau. Is not the soft air of your native south.
How pale he is ! indeed thou art not well.
Where are our people ? I will call them.

Mel.   Hold !
I—I am well.

Pau.   Thou art !—Ah ! now I know it.
Thou fanciest, my kind lord, I know thou dost,

Thou fanciest these rude walls, these rustic gossips,
Brick'd floors, sour wine, coarse viands, vex Pauline ;
And so they might, but thou art by my side,
And I forget all else !   Nay, let it not
Chafe thee, sweet prince !   A few short days, and we
Shall see thy palace by its lake of silver,
And—nay, nay, spendthrift, is thy wealth of smiles
Already drain'd, or dost thou play the miser ?
   Mel. Thine eyes would call up smiles in deserts, fair one.
Let us escape these rustics : close at hand
There is a cot, where I have bid prepare
Our evening lodgement ; a rude, homely roof,
But honest, where our welcome will not be
Made torture by the vulgar eyes and tongues
That are as death to Love !   A heavenly night !
The wooing air and the soft moon invite us.
Wilt walk ?   I pray thee, now,—I know the path,
Ay, every inch of it !
   Pau.   What, *thou !* methought
Thou wert a stranger in these parts.   Ah, truant,
Some village beauty lured thee ; thou art now
Grown constant ?
   Mel.   Trust me.
   Pau.   Princes are so changeful !
   Mel. Come, dearest, come.
   Pau.   Shall I not call our people
To light us ?
   Mel.   Heaven will lend its stars for torches !
It is not far.
   Pau.   The night breeze chills me.
   Mel.   Nay.
Let me thus mantle thee ; it is not cold.
   Pau. Never beneath thy smile !
   Mel.   [*Aside*] O heaven ! forgive me !
                              [*Exeunt.*

SCENE II. *Melnotte's cottage. A table spread for supper.*
Widow *bustling about.*

Wid. So, I think that looks very neat. He sent me a line so blotted that I can scarcely read it, to say he would be here almost immediately. She must have loved him well indeed to have forgotten his birth ; for though he was introduced to her in disguise, he is too honourable not to have revealed to her the artifice, which her love only could forgive. Well, I do not wonder at it ; for though my son is not a prince, he ought to be one, and that's almost as good. [*Knock at the door.*] Ah! here they are.

Enter MELNOTTE *and* PAULINE.

Wid. Oh, my boy, the pride of my heart! welcome, welcome ! I beg pardon, ma'am, but I do love him so!

Pau. Good woman, I really—why, prince, what is this ? does the old lady know you ? Oh, I guess you have done her some service. Another proof of your kind heart ; is it not ?

Mel. Of my kind heart, ay !

Pau. So, you know the prince ?

Wid. Know him, madam ? Ah, I begin to fear it is you who know him not !

Pau. Do you think she is mad ? Can we stay here, my lord ? I think there's something very wild about her.

Mel. Madam, I—no, I cannot tell her ; my knees knock together : what a coward is a man who has lost his honour ! Speak to her, speak to her [*To his mother*] tell her that—O heaven, that I were dead !

Pau. How confused he looks ! this strange place, this woman, what can it mean ? I half suspect. Who are you, madam ! who are you ? can't you speak ? are you struck dumb ?

Wid. Claude, you have not deceived her ? Ah, shame upon you ! I thought that, before you went to the altar, she was to have known all ?

Pau. All ! what ? My blood freezes in my veins !

Wid. Poor lady! Dare I tell her, Claude? [*Melnotte makes a sign of assent.*] Know you not then, madam, that this young man is of poor though honest parents? Know you not that you are wedded to my son, Claude Melnotte?

Pau. Your son! hold! hold! do not speak to me. [*Approaches Melnotte and lays her hand on his arm.*] Is this a jest? is it? I know it is; only speak, one word, one look, one smile. I cannot believe, I, who loved thee so, I cannot believe that thou art such a—No, I will not wrong thee by a harsh word. Speak!

Mel. Leave us; have pity on her, on me: leave us.

Wid. Oh, Claude! that I should live to see the bowed by shame! thee, of whom I was so proud! [*Exit by the staircase.*

Pau. Her son! her son!

Mel.   Now, lady, hear me.

Pau.   Hear thee!
Ay, speak. Her son! have fiends a parent? speak,
That thou mayst silence curses. Speak!

Mel.   No, curse me:
Thy curse would blast me less than thy forgiveness.

Pau. [*Laughing wildly*] 'This is thy palace, where the per-
                fumed light
Steals through the mist of alabaster lamps,
And every air is heavy with the sighs
Of orange-groves, and music from sweet lutes,
And murmurs of low fountains, that gush forth
I' the midst of roses!' Dost thou like the picture?
This is my bridal home, and *thou* my bridegroom.
O fool! O dupe! O wretch! I see it all;
The by-word and the jeer of every tongue
In Lyons! Hast thou in thy heart one touch
Of human kindness? if thou hast, why, kill me,
And save thy wife from madness. No, it cannot,
It cannot be: this is some horrid dream:
I shall wake soon. [*Touching him*] Art flesh? art man? or but

The shadows seen in sleep? It is too real.
What have I done to thee? how sinn'd against thee,
That thou shouldst crush me thus?
 Mel.   Pauline, by pride
Angels have fallen ere thy time : by pride,
That sole alloy of thy most lovely mould,
The evil spirit of a bitter love,
And a revengeful heart, had power upon thee.
From my first years my soul was fill'd with thee :
I saw thee midst the flow'rs the lowly boy
Tended, unmark'd by thee, a spirit of bloom,
And joy and freshness, as if Spring itself
Were made a living thing, and wore thy shape !
I saw thee, and the passionate heart of man
Enter'd the breast of the wild-dreaming boy.
And from that hour I grew, what to the last
I shall be, thine adorer! Well! this love,
Vain, frantic, guilty, if thou wilt, became
A fountain of ambition and bright hope ;
I thought of tales that by the winter hearth
Old gossips tell, how maidens sprung from kings,
Have stoop'd from their high sphere ; how love, like death,
Levels all ranks, and lays the shepherd's crook
Beside the sceptre. Thus I made my home
In the soft palace of a fairy Future !
My father died ; and I, the peasant-born,
Was my own lord. Then did I seek to rise
Out of the prison of my mean estate ;
And, with such jewels as the exploring mind
Brings from the caves of knowledge, buy my ransom
From those twin gaolers of the daring heart,
Low birth and iron fortune. Thy bright image
Glass'd in my soul, took all the hues of glory,
And lured me on to those inspiring toils
By which man masters men ! For thee I grew

A midnight student o'er the dreams of sages :
For thee I sought to borrow from each grace,
And every muse, such attributes as lend
Ideal charms to love. I thought of thee,
And passion taught me poesy, of thee,
And on the painter's canvas grew the life
Of beauty ! Art became the shadow
Of the dear starlight of thy haunting eyes !
Men call'd me vain, some mad, I heeded not,
But still toil'd on, hoped on, for it was sweet,
If not to win, to feel more worthy thee !

 Pau. [*Aside*] Has he a magic to exorcise hate ?

 Mel. At last, in one mad hour, I dared to pour
The thoughts that burst their channels into song,
And sent them to thee, such a tribute, lady,
As beauty rarely scorns, even from the meanest.
The name, appended by the burning heart
That long'd to show its idol what bright things
It had created ; yea, the enthusiast's name,
That should have been thy triumph, was thy scorn!
That very hour, when passion, turned to wrath,
Resembled hatred most ; when thy disdain
Made my whole soul a chaos ; in that hour
The tempters found me a revengeful tool
For their revenge ! Thou hadst trampled on the worm,
It turn'd and stung thee !

 Pau.   Love, sir, hath no sting.
What was the slight of a poor powerless girl
To the deep wrong of this most vile revenge ?
Oh, how I loved this man ! a serf ! a slave !

 Mel. Hold, lady ! No, not slave ! Despair is free !
I will not tell thee of the throes, the struggles,
The anguish, the remorse : No, let it pass !
And let me come to such most poor atonement

Yet in my power.   Pauline!—[*Approaching her with great emo-*
                                    tion, and about to take her hand.
    Pau.   No, touch me not!
I know my fate.   You are, by law, my tyrant;
And I, O heaven! a peasant's wife!   I'll work,
Toil, drudge, do what thou wilt; but touch me not:
Let my wrongs make me sacred!
    Mel.   Do not fear me.
Thou dost not know me, madam: at the altar
My vengeance ceased, my guilty oath expired!
Henceforth, no image of some marble saint,
Niched in cathedral aisles, is hallow'd more
From the rude hand of sacrilegious wrong.
I am thy husband; nay, thou need'st not shudder:
Here, at thy feet, I lay a husband's rights.
A marriage thus unholy, unfulfill'd,
A bond of fraud, is, by the laws of France,
Made void and null.   To-night, sleep, sleep in peace.
To-morrow, pure and virgin as this morn
I bore thee, bathed in blushes, from the shrine,
Thy father's arms shall take thee to thy home.
The law shall do thee justice, and restore
Thy right to bless another with thy love.
And when thou art happy, and hast half forgot
Him who so loved, so wrong'd thee, think at least
Heaven left some remnant of the angel still
In that poor peasant's nature!   Ho! my mother!

Enter Widow.

Conduct this lady—she is not my wife;
She is our guest, our honour'd guest, my mother—
To the poor chamber where the sleep of virtue
Never beneath my father's honest roof,
E'en villains dared to mar!   Now, lady, now,
I think thou wilt believe me.   Go, my mother.

Wid. She is not thy wife !

Mel.　　　　　 ¯ Hush ! hush ! for mercy sake !
Speak not, but go.　　　*[Widow ascends the stairs ; Pauline follows
　　　　　　　　　　　　　　　weeping—turns to look back.*

Mel. [*Sinking down*] All angels bless and guard her !
　　　　　　　　　　　　　　　　　　　 [The curtain falls.

ACT IV.

SCENE I. *The Cottage as before.   Day breaking.*
MELNOTTE *seated before a table—writing implements, &c.*

Mel. Hush, hush ! she sleeps at last ! thank heaven, for
a while she forgets even that I live !   Her sobs, which have gone
to my heart the whole, long desolate night, have ceased ! all
calm, all still !   I will go now ; I will send this letter to Pauline's
father : when he arrives, I will place in his hands my own consent to the divorce, and then, O France ! my country ! accept
among thy protectors, thy defenders, the Peasant's Son !   Our
country is less proud than custom, and does not refuse the blood,
the heart, the right hand of the poor man !

Enter Widow.

Wid. My son, thou hast acted ill ; but sin brings its own punishment.   In the hour of thy remorse, it is not for a mother to
reproach thee.

Mel. What is past is past.   There is a future left to all men,
who have the virtue to repent, and the energy to atone.   Thou
shalt be proud of thy son yet.   Meanwhile, remember this poor
lady has been grievously injured.   For the sake of thy son's conscience, respect, honour, bear with her.   If she weep, console ;
if she chide, be silent.   'Tis but a little while more ; I shall
send an express fast as horse can speed to her father.   Farewell !   I shall return shortly.

Wid. It is the only course left to thee ; thou wert led astray,

but thou art not hardened.   Thy heart is right still, as ever it
was, when, in thy most ambitious hopes, thou wert never ashamed
of thy poor mother.

Mel. Ashamed of thee!   No, if I yet endure, yet live, yet
hope, it is only because I would not die till I have redeemed the
noble heritage I have lost, the heritage I took unstained from thee
and my dead father, a proud conscience and an honest name.   I
shall win them back yet.   Heaven bless you.   [*Exit.*

Wid. My dear Claude! How my heart bleeds for him!

PAULINE *looks down from above, and after a pause descends.*

Pau. Not here! he spares me that pain at least: so far he is
considerate, yet the place seems still more desolate without him.
Oh, that I could hate him; the gardener's son! and yet how
nobly he—no, no, no, I will not be so mean a thing as to forgive
him!

Wid. Good morning, madam; I would have waited on you
if I had known you were stirring.

Pau. It is no matter, ma'am; your son's wife ought to wait on
herself.

Wid. My son's wife! let not that thought vex you, madam;
he tells me that you will have your divorce.   And I hope I
shall live to see him smile again.   There are maidens in this village, young and fair, madam, who may yet console him.

Pau. I dare say, they are very welcome; and when the
divorce is got, he will marry again.   I am sure I hope so.   [*Weeps.*

Wid. He could have married the richest girl in the province,
if he had pleased it; but his head was turned, poor child! he
could think of nothing but you.   [*Weeps.*

Pau. Don't weep, *mother!*

Wid. Ah, he has behaved very ill, I know, but love is so
headstrong in the young.   Don't weep, madam.

Pau. So, as you was saying; go on.

Wid. Oh, I cannot excuse him, ma'am; he was not in his
right senses.

Pau. But he always—always—[*Sobbing*] loved—loved me then?

Wid. He thought of nothing else.   See here, he learnt to paint that he might take your likeness. [*Uncovers the picture.*] But that's all over now ; I trust you have cured him of his folly. But, dear heart you have had no breakfast.

Pau. I can't take anything, don't trouble yourself.

Wid. Nay, madam, be persuaded ; a little coffee will refresh you.   Our milk and eggs are excellent.   I will get out Claude's coffee-cup, it is of real Sèvres ; he saved up all his money to buy it three years ago, because the name of *Pauline* was inscribed on it.

Pau. Three years ago !   Poor Claude !   Thank you ; I think I will have some coffee.   Oh, if he were but a poor gentleman, even a merchant : but a gardener's son ! and what a home !   Oh no, it is too dreadful.   [*They seat themselves at the table, Beauseant opens the lattice and looks in.*

Beau. So, so, the coast is clear !   I saw Claude in the lane ; I shall have an excellent opportunity.

[*Shuts the lattice and knocks at the door.*

Pau. [*Starting*] Can it be my father ?   He has not sent for him yet ?   No, he cannot be in such a hurry to get rid of me.

Wid. It is not time for your father to arrive yet ; it must be some neighbour.

Pau. Don't admit any one.   [*Widow opens the door.*

BEAUSEANT *pushes her aside and enters.*

Ha ! heavens ! that hateful Beauseant !   This is indeed bitter.

Beau. Good morning, madam !   O widow, your son begs you will have the goodness to go to him in the village, he wants to speak to you on particular business ; you will find him at the inn, or the grocer's shop, or the baker's, or at some other friend's of your family, make haste !

Pau. Don't leave me, mother !   don't leave me !

Beau. [*With great respect*]   Be not alarmed, madam.   Believe me your friend, your servant.

Pau. Sir, I have no fear of you, even in this house! Go, madam, if your son wishes it ; I will not contradict his commands whilst at least he has still the right to be obeyed.

Wid. I don't understand this ; however, I shan't be long gone.

[*Exit.*

Pau. Sir, I divine the object of your visit, you wish to exult in the humiliation of one who humbled you. Be it so ; I am prepared to endure all, even your presence !

Beau. You mistake me, madam, Pauline, you mistake me! I come to lay my fortune at your feet. You must already be disenchanted with this impostor ; these walls are not worthy to be hallowed by your beauty! Shall that form be clasped in the arms of a base-born peasant ? Beloved, beautiful Pauline! fly with me, my carriage waits without, I will bear you to a home more meet for your reception. Wealth, luxury, station, all shall yet be yours. I forget your past disdain, I remember only your beauty and my unconquerable love !

Pau. Sir ! leave this house ; it is humble : but a husband's roof, however lowly, is, in the eyes of God and man, the temple of a wife's honour ! Know that I would rather starve, yes, with him who has betrayed me, than accept your lawful hand, even were you the prince whose name he bore ! Go !

Beau. What, is not your pride humbled yet ?

Pau. Sir, what was pride in prosperity, in affliction becomes virtue.

Beau. Look round : these rugged floors, these homely walls, this wretched struggle of poverty for comfort, think of this ! and contrast with such a picture the refinement, the luxury, the pomp, that the wealthiest gentleman of Lyons offers to the loveliest lady. Ah, hear me !

Pau. Oh! my father! why did I leave you? why am I thus friendless ? Sir, you see before you a betrayed, injured, miserable woman ! respect her anguish !

MELNOTTE *opens the door silently and pauses at the threshold.*

Beau. No! let me rather thus console it ; let me snatch from those lips one breath of that fragrance which never should be wasted on the low churl thy husband.

Pau. Help! Claude! Claude! Have I no protector?

Beau. Be silent! [*Showing a pistol*] See, I do not come unprepared even for violence. I will brave all things, thy husband and all his race, for thy sake. Thus, then, I clasp thee!

Mel. [*Dashing him to the other end of the stage*] Pauline, look up, Pauline! thou art safe.

Beau. [*Levelling his pistol*] Dare you thus insult a man of my birth, ruffian?

Pau. Oh, spare him, spare my husband! Beauseant—Claude —no—no—   [*Faints.*

Mel. Miserable trickster! shame upon you! brave devices to terrify a woman! Coward, you tremble, you have outraged the laws, you know that your weapon is harmless, you have the courage of the mountebank, not the bravo! Pauline, there is no danger.

Beau. I wish thou wert a gentleman, as it is, thou art beneath me. Good day, and a happy honey-moon. [*Aside*] I will not die till I am avenged.   [*Exit.*

Mel. I hold her in these arms, the last embrace!
Never, ah never more, shall this dear head
Be pillow'd on the heart that should have shelter'd
And has betray'd! Soft, soft! one kiss, poor wretch!
No scorn on that pale lip forbids me now!
One kiss, so ends all record of my crime!
It is the seal upon the tomb of hope,
By which, like some lost, sorrowing angel, sits
Sad memory evermore: she breathes, she moves,
She wakes to scorn, to hate, but not to shudder
Beneath the touch of my abhorred love.   [*Places her on a seat.*
There, we are strangers now!

Pau.   All gone, all calm,
Is *every* thing a dream? thou art safe, unhurt:
I do not love thee; but—but I am a woman.
And—and—no blood is spilt?

Mel.   No, lady, no;
My guilt has not deserved so rich a blessing
As even danger in thy cause.

Re-enter Widow.

Wid. My son, I have been everywhere in search of you; why
did you send for me?

Mel. I did not send for you.

Wid. No! but I must tell you your express has returned.

Mel. So soon! impossible!

Wid. Yes, he met the lady's father and mother on the road;
they were going into the country on a visit. Your messenger
says that Monsieur Deschappelles turned almost white with anger
when he read your letter. They will be here almost immediately.
Oh, Claude, Claude! what will they do to you? How I tremble! Ah, madam! do not let them injure him; if you knew
how he doated on you!

Pau. Injure him! no ma'am, be not afraid; my father! how
shall I meet him? how go back to Lyons? the scoff of the whole
city! Cruel, cruel, Claude! [*In great agitation*] Sir, you have
acted most treacherously.

Mel. I know it, madam.

Pau. [*Aside*] If he would but ask me to forgive him! [*Aloud*]
I never can forgive you, sir.

Mel. I never dared to hope it.

Pau. But you are my husband now, and I have sworn to—to
love you, sir.

Mel. That was under a false belief, madam; heaven and the
laws will release you from your vow.

Pau. He will drive me mad! if he were but less proud, if he
would but ask me to remain—hark, hark! I hear the wheels of
the carriage; Sir—Claude, they are coming; have you no word
to say ere it is too late? quick, speak!

Mel. I can only congratulate you on your release. Behold
your parents!

Enter MONSIEUR *and* MADAME DESCHAPPELLES *and* COLONEL DAMAS.

M. Des. My child ! my child !

Mme. D. Oh, my poor Pauline ! what a villainous hovel this is ! Old woman, get me a chair, I shall faint, I certainly shall. What will the world say ? Child, you have been a fool. A mother's heart is easily broken.

Dam. Ha, ha ! most noble prince, I am sorry to see a man of your quality in such a condition ; I am afraid your highness will go'to the House of Correction.

Mel. Taunt on, sir ; I spared *you* when you were unarmed, I am unarmed now. A man who has no excuse for crime is indeed defenceless !

Dam. There's something fine in the rascal, after all !

M. Des. Where is the impostor ? Are you thus shameless, traitor ? Can you brave the presence of that girl's father ?

Mel. Strike me, if it please you, you *are* her father !

Pau. Sir, sir, for my sake ; whatever his guilt, he has acted nobly in atonement.

Mme. D. Nobly ! Are you mad girl ? I have no patience with you, to disgrace all your family thus ! Nobly ! Oh you abominable, hardened, pitiful, mean, ugly villain !

Dam. Ugly ! Why he was beautiful yesterday.

Pau. Madam, this is his roof, and he is my husband. Respect your daughter, and let blame fall alone on her.

Mme. D. You—you—Oh, I'm choking.

M. Des. Sir, it were idle to waste reproach upon a conscience like yours, you renounce all pretensions to the person of this lady ?

Mel. I do. [*Gives a paper.*] Here is my consent to a divorce, my full confession of the fraud, which annuls marriage. Your daughter has been foully wronged, I grant it, sir ; but her own lips will tell you that, from the hour in which she crossed this threshold, I returned to my own station, and respected hers. Pure and inviolate, as when yestermorn you laid your hand upon

her head and blessed her, I yield her back to you.   For myself, I
deliver you for ever from my presence.   An outcast and a criminal, I seek some distant land, where I may mourn my sin, and
pray for your daughter's peace.   Farewell, farewell to you all
for ever!

Wid. Claude, Claude, you will not leave your poor mother?
She does not disown you in your sorrow, no, not even in your
guilt.   No divorce can separate a mother from her son.

Pau. This poor widow teaches me my duty.   No, mother, no,
for you are now *my* mother also! nor should any law, human or
divine, separate the wife from her husband's sorrows.   Claude,
Claude, all is forgotten, forgiven, I am thine for ever!

Mme. D. What do I hear? Come away, or never see my
face again.

M. Des. Pauline, *we* never betrayed you! do you forsake us
for him?

Pau. [*Going back to her father*] Oh no! but you will forgive
him, too ; we will live together—he shall be your son.

M. Des. Never! Cling to him and forsake your parents!
His home shall be yours, his fortune yours, his fate yours: the
wealth I have acquired by honest industry shall never enrich the
dishonest man.

Pau. And you would have a wife enjoy luxury while a husband
toils! Claude, take me ; thou canst not give me wealth, titles,
station, but thou canst give me a true heart.   I will work for
thee, tend thee, bear with thee, and never, never shall these lips
reproach thee for the past.

Dam. I'll be hanged if I am not going to blubber!

Mel. This is the heaviest blow of all! What a heart I have
wronged! Do not fear me, sir ; I am not all hardened ; I
will not rob her of a holier love than mine.   Pauline! angel of
love and mercy! your memory shall lead me back to virtue!
The husband of a being so beautiful in her noble and sublime
tenderness may be poor, may be low-born,—there is no guilt in
the decrees of Providence !—but he should be one who can look

thee in the face without a blush, to whom thy love does not bring remorse, who can fold thee to his heart and say, ' *Here* there is no deceit !'—I am not that man !

Dam. [*Aside to Melnotte*] Thou art a noble fellow, notwithstanding, and wouldst make an excellent soldier. Serve in my regiment. I have had a letter from the Directory, our young general takes the command of the army in Italy ; I am to join him at Marseilles, I will depart this day if·thou wilt go with me.

Mel. It is the favour I would have asked thee, if I dared. Place me wherever a foe is most dreaded, wherever France most needs a life !

Dam. There shall not be forlorn hope without thee !

Mel. There is my hand ! Mother ! your blessing ; I shall see you again, a better man than a prince, a man who has bought the right to high thoughts by brave deeds. And thou ! thou ! so wildly worshipped, so guiltily betrayed, all is not yet lost ! for thy memory, at least, must be mine till death ! If I live, the name of him thou hast once loved shall not rest dishonoured ; if I fall, amidst the carnage and the roar of battle, my soul will fly back to thee, and Love shall share with Death my last sigh ! More, more would I speak to thee ! to pray ! to bless ! But no ! when I am less unworthy I will utter it to heaven ! I cannot trust myself to—[*Turning to Deschappelles*] Your pardon, sir ; they are my last words. Farewell ! [*The curtain falls.*

ACT V.

[Two years and a half from the date of Act IV.]

SCENE I. *The streets of Lyons.*

Enter First, Second, *and* Third Officers.

First Off. Well, here we are at Lyons, with gallant old Damas : it is his native place.

3

Sec. Off. Yes; he has gained a step in the army since he was here last. The Lyonnese ought to be very proud of stout General Damas.

Third Off. Promotion is quick in the French army. This mysterious Morier, the hero of Lodi, and the favourite of the commander-in-chief, has risen to a colonel's rank in two years and a half.

Enter DAMAS, *as a General.*

Dam. Good morrow, gentlemen; I hope you will amuse yourselves during our short stay at Lyons. It is a fine city: improved since I left it. Ah! it is a pleasure to grow old, when the years that bring decay to ourselves do but ripen the prosperity of our country. You have not met with Morier?

First Off. No: we were just speaking of him.

Sec. Off. Pray, general, can you tell us who this Morier really is?

Dam. Is? why a colonel in the French army.

Third Off. True. But what was he at first?

Dam. At first? Why a baby in long clothes, I suppose.

First Off. Ha, ha! Ever facetious, general.

Sec. Off. [*To Third*] The general is sore upon this point; you will only chafe him. Any commands, general?

Dam. None. Good day to you!

[*Exeunt Second and Third Officers.*

Dam. Our comrades are very inquisitive. Poor Morier is the subject of a vast deal of curiosity.

First Off. Say interest, rather, general. His constant melancholy, the loneliness of his habits, his daring valour, his brilliant rise in the profession, your friendship, and the favours of the commander-in-chief, all tend to make him as much the matter of gossip as of admiration. But where is he, general? I have missed him all the morning.

Dam. Why, captain, I'll let you into a secret. My young friend has come with me to Lyons in hopes of finding a miracle.

First Off. A miracle!

Dam. Yes, a miracle! in other words, a constant woman.

First Off. Oh! an affair of love!

Dam. Exactly so. No sooner did he enter Lyons than he waved his hand to me, threw himself from his horse, and is now, I warrant, asking every one who can know anything about the matter, whether a certain lady is still true to a certain gentleman!

First Off. Success to him! and of that success there can be no doubt. The gallant Colonel Morier, the hero of Lodi, might make his choice out of the proudest families in France.

Dam. Oh, if pride be a recommendation, the lady and her mother are most handsomely endowed. By the way, captain, if you should chance to meet with Morier, tell him he will find me at the hotel.

First Off. I will, general.   [*Exit.*

Dam. Now will I go to the Deschappelles, and make a report to my young colonel. Ha! by Mars, Bacchus, Apollo, Virorum, here comes Monsieur Beauseant.

Enter BEAUSEANT.

Good morrow, Monsieur Beauseant! How fares it with you?

Beau. [*Aside*] Damas! that is unfortunate; if the Italian campaign should have filled his pockets, he may seek to baffle me in the moment of my victory. [*Aloud*] Your servant, general, for such, I think, is your new distinction! Just arrived in Lyons?

Dam. Not an hour ago. Well, how go on the Deschappelles? Have they forgiven you in that affair of young Melnotte? You had some hand in that notable device, eh?

Beau. Why, less than you think for! The fellow imposed upon me. I have set it all right now. What has become of him? He could not have joined the army, after all. There is no such name in the books.

Dam. I know nothing about Melnotte. As you say, I never heard the name in the Grand Army.

Beau. Hem! You are not married, general?

Dam. Do I look like a married man, sir? No, thank heaven! My profession is to make widows, not wives.

Beau. You must have gained much booty in Italy! Pauline will be your heiress, eh?

Dam. Booty! Not I! Heiress to what? Two trunks and a portmanteau, four horses, three swords, two suits of regiment-als, and six pair of white leather inexpressibles! A pretty for-tune for a young lady!

Beau. [*Aside*] Then all is safe! [*Aloud*] Ha! ha! Is that really all your capital, General Damas? Why, I thought Italy had been a second Mexico to you soldiers.

Dam. All a toss-up, sir. I was not one of the lucky ones! My friend Morier, indeed, saved something handsome. But our commander-in-chief took care of him, and Morier is a thrifty, economical dog, not like the rest of us soldiers, who spend our money as carelessly as if it were our blood.

Beau. Well, it is no matter! I do not want fortune with Pauline. And you must know, General Damas, that your fair cousin has at length consented to reward my long and ardent attachment.

Dam. You! the devil! Why, she is already married. There is no divorce.

Beau. True; but this very day she is formally to authorize the necessary proceedings, this very day she is to sign the contract that is to make her mine within one week from the day on which her present illegal marriage is annulled.

Dam. You tell me wonders! Wonders! No; I believe anything of women!

Beau. I must wish you good morning.   [*As he is going*

Enter DESCHAPPELLES.

M. Des. Oh, Beauseant! well met. Let us come to the notary at once.   [*Going.*

Dam. [*To Deschappelles*] Why, cousin?   [*Exit Beauseant.*

M. Des. Damas, welcome to Lyons.   Pray call on us ; my wife will be delighted to see you.

Dam. Your wife be —— blessed for her condescension !   But [*Taking him aside*] what do I hear ?   Is it possible that your daughter has consented to a divorce ? that she will marry Monsieur Beauseant ?

M. Des. Certainly !   What have you to say against it ?   A gentleman of birth, fortune character.   We are not so proud as we were ; even my wife has had enough of nobility and princes !

Dam. But Pauline loved that young man so tenderly.

M. Des. [*Taking snuff*] That was two years and a half ago.

Dam. Very true.   Poor Melnotte !

M. Des. But do not talk of that impostor ; I hope he is dead or has left the country.   Nay, even were he in Lyons at this moment, he ought to rejoice that, in an honourable and suitable alliance, my daughter may forget her suffering and his crime.

Dam. Nay, if it be all settled I have no more to say.   Monsieur Beauseant informs me that the contract is to be signed this very day.

M. Des. It is ; at one o'clock precisely.   Will you be one of the witnesses ?

Dam. I ?   No ; that is to say, yes, certainly ! at one o'clock I will wait on you.

M. Des. Till then, adieu.   [*Exit.*

Dam. The man who sets his heart upon a woman
Is a chameleon, and doth feed on air ;
From air he takes his colours, holds his life,
Changes with every wind, grows lean or fat,
Rosy with hope, or green with jealousy,
Or pallid with despair, just as the gale
Varies from north to south, from heat to cold !
Oh, woman ! woman ! thou shouldst have few sins
Of thine own to answer for !   Thou art the author
Of such a book of follies in a man,

That it would need the tears of all the angels
To blot the record out!

Enter MELNOTTE, *pale and agitated.*

I need not tell thee! Thou hast heard—
    Mel.   The worst!
I have!
    Dam. Be cheer'd; others are fair as she is!
    Mel. Others! The world is crumbled at my feet!
She *was* my world; fill'd up the whole of being,
Smiled in the sunshine, walk'd the glorious earth,
Sate in my heart, was the sweet life of life:
The Past was hers; I dreamt not of a Future
That did not wear her shape! Mem'ry and Hope
Alike are gone. Pauline is faithless! Henceforth
The universal space is desolate!
    Dam. Hope yet.
    Mel.   Hope? yes! one hope is left me still,
A soldier's grave! Glory has died with love.
I look into my heart, and, where I saw
Pauline, see Death!
[*After a pause.*] But am I not deceived?
I went but by the rumour of the town;
Rumour is false,—I was too hasty! Damas,
Whom hast thou seen?
    Dam.   Thy rival and her father.
Arm thyself for the truth! He heeds not—
    Mel.   She
Will never know how deeply she was loved!
The charitable night, that wont to bring
Comfort to-day, in bright and eloquent dreams,
Is henceforth leagued with misery! Sleep, farewell,
Or else become eternal! Oh, the waking
From false oblivion, to see the sun,
And know she is another's!

Dam.   Be a man!

Mel. I am a man! it is the sting of woe
Like mine that tells us we are men!

Dam.   The false one
Did not deserve thee.

Mel.   Hush! No word against her!
Why should she keep, through years and silent absence,
The holy tablets of her virgin faith
True to a traitor's name? Oh, blame her not;
It were a sharper grief to think her worthless
Than to be what I am! To-day, to-day!
They said 'to-day!' This day, so wildly welcomed,
This day, my soul had singled out of time
And mark'd for bliss! This day! oh, could I see her,
See her once more unknown; hear but her voice,
So that one echo of its music might
Make ruin less appalling in its silence!

Dam. Easily done! Come with me to her house;
Your dress, your cloak, moustache, the bronzed hues
Of time and toil, the name you bear, belief
In your absence, all will ward away suspicion.
Keep in the shade. Ay, I would have you come.
There may be hope! Pauline is yet so young,
They may have forced her to these second bridals
Out of mistaken love.

Mel.   No, bid me hope not!
Bid me not hope! I could not bear again
To fall from such a heaven! One gleam of sunshine,
And the ice breaks, and I am lost! Oh, Damas,
There's no such thing as courage in a man;
The veriest slave that ever crawl'd from danger
Might spurn me now. When first I lost her, Damas,
I bore it, did I not? I still had hope,
And now I—I—   [*Bursts into an agony of grief.*

Dam.   What, comrade! all the women

That ever smiled destruction on brave hearts
Were not worth tears like these!

Mel.   'Tis past, forget it.
I am prepared; life has no farther ills!
The cloud has broken in that stormy rain,
And on the waste I stand, alone with heaven!

Dam. His very face is changed ; a breaking heart
Does its work soon!   Come, Melnotte, rouse thyself:
One effort more.   Again thou'lt see her.

Mel.   See her!
There is a passion in that simple sentence
That shivers all the pride and power of reason
Into a chaos!

Dam.   Time wanes ; come, ere yet
It be too late.

Mel.   Terrible words. ' *Too late!*'
Lead on.   One last look more, and then—

Dam.   Forget her!

Mel. Forget her, yes!   For death remembers not.   [*Exeunt.*

SCENE II.   *A room in the house of Monsieur Deschappelles.*
        PAULINE *seated in great dejection.*

Pau. It is so, then.   I must be false to love,
Or sacrifice a father!   Oh, my Claude,
My lover and my husband! have I lived
To pray that thou mayst find some fairer boon
Than the deep faith of this devoted heart,
Nourish'd till now, now broken!

                Enter DESCHAPPELLES.

M. Des.   My dear child,
How shall I thank, how bless thee ?   Thou hast saved,
I will not say my fortune, I could bear
Reverse, and shrink not, but that prouder wealth

Which merchants value most, my name, my credit,
The hard-won honours of a toilsome life :
These thou hast saved, my child !
    Pau.   Is there no hope ?
No hope but this ?
    M. Des.   None.   If, without the sum
Which Beauseant offers for thy hand, this day
Sinks to the west, to-morrow brings our ruin !
And hundreds, mingled in that ruin, curse
The bankrupt merchant ! and the insolent herd
We feasted and made merry, cry in scorn,
' How pride has fallen !   Lo, the bankrupt merchant !'
My daughter, thou hast saved us !
    Pau.   And am lost !
    M. Des. Come, let me hope that Beauseant's love—
    Pau.   His love !
Talk not of love.   Love has no thought of self !
Love buys not with the ruthless usurer's gold
The loathsome prostitution of a hand
Without a heart !   Love sacrifices all things,
To bless the thing it loves !   *He* knows not love.
Father, his love is hate, his hope revenge !
My tears, my anguish, my remorse for falsehood,
'These are the joys he wrings from our despair !
    M. Des. If thou deem'st thus, reject him !   Shame and ruin
Were better than thy misery ; think no more on't.
My sand is well-nigh run, what boots it when
The glass is broken ?   We'll annul the contract ;
And if to-morrow in the prisoner's cell
These aged limbs are laid, why still, my child,
I'll think thou art spared ; and wait the liberal hour
That lays the beggar by the side of kings !
    Pau. No ! no ! forgive me !   You, my honour'd father,
You, who so loved, so cherish'd me, whose lips
Never knew one harsh word !   I'm not ungrateful ;

    :*

I am but human! hush! *Now*, call the bridegroom,
You see I am prepared, no tears, all calm ;
But, father, *talk no more of love!*
    M. Des.   My child,
'Tis but one struggle ; he is young, rich, noble ;
Thy state will rank first 'mid the dames of Lyons ;
And when this heart can shelter thee no more,
Thy youth will not be guardianless.
    Pau.   I have set
My foot upon the ploughshare, I will pass
The fiery ordeal. [*Aside*] Merciful heaven, support me !
And on the absent wanderer shed the light
Of happier stars, lost ever more to me !

Enter MADAME DESCHAPPELLES, BEAUSEANT, GLAVIS *and*
                  Notary.

    Mme. D. Why, Pauline, you are quite in *déshabille*, you ought
to be more alive to the importance of this joyful occasion. We
had once looked higher, it is true ; but, you see, after all, Monsieur Beauseant's father *was* a marquess, and that's a great comfort ! Pedigree and jointure ! you have them both in Monsieur
Beauseant. A young lady decorously brought up should only
have two considerations in her choice of a husband : first, is his
birth honourable ? secondly, will his death be advantageous ? _
All other trifling details should be left to parental anxiety.
    Beau. [*Approaching and waving aside Madame*] Ah Pauline !
let me hope that you are reconciled to an event which confers
such rapture upon me.
    Pau. I am reconciled to my doom.
    Beau. Doom is a harsh word, sweet lady.
    Pau. [*Aside*] This man must have some mercy, his heart can-
not be marble. [*Aloud*] Oh, sir, be just, be generous ! Seize a
noble triumph, a great revenge ! Save the father, and spare the child !
    Beau. [*Aside*] Joy, joy alike to my hatred and my passion !
The haughty Pauline is at last my suppliant. [*Aloud*] You ask

from me what I have not the sublime virtue to grant, a virtue reserved only for the gardener's son ! I cannot forego my hopes in the moment of their fulfilment ! I adhere to the contract, your father's ruin, or your hand !

Pau. Then all is over. Sir, I have decided.

[*The clock strikes one.*

Enter DAMAS *and* MELNOTTE.

Dam. Your servant, cousin Deschappelles. Let me introduce Colonel Morier.

Mme. D. [*Curtseying very low*] What, the celebrated hero? This is, indeed, an honour.

[*Melnotte bows, and remains in the background.*

Dam. [*To Pauline*] My little cousin, I congratulate you! What, no smile, no blush? You are going to be divorced from poor Melnotte, and marry this rich gentleman. You ought to be excessively happy !

Pau. Happy !

Dam. Why, how pale you are, child ! Poor Pauline ! Hist, confide in me ! Do they force you to this?

Pau. No !

Dam. You act with your own free consent ?

Pau. My own consent, yes.

Dam. Then you are the most—I will not say what you are.

Pau. You think ill of me, be it so, yet if you knew all—

Dam. There is some mystery, speak out, Pauline.

Pau. [*Suddenly*] Oh, perhaps you can save me ! you are our relation, our friend. My father is on the verge of bankruptcy, this day he requires a large sum to meet demands that cannot be denied ; that sum Beauseant will advance, this hand the condition of the barter. Save me if you have the means, save me ! You will be repaid above !

Dam. [*Aside*] I recant ; women are not so bad after all ! [*Aloud*] Hum, child ! I cannot help you, I am too poor.

Pau. The last plank to which I clung is shivered.

Dam. Hold, you see my friend Morier: Melnotte is his most intimate friend, fought in the same fields—slept in the same tent. Have you any message to send to Melnotte? any word to soften this blow?

Pau. He knows Melnotte, he will see him, he will bear to him my last farewell. [*Approaches Melnotte*] He has a stern air, he turns away from me—he despises me! Sir, one word I beseech you.

Mel. Her voice again! How the old time comes o'er me!

Dam. [*To Madame*] Don't interrupt them. He is going to tell her what a rascal young Melnotte is; he knows him well, I promise you.

Mme. D. So considerate in you, cousin Damas!

> [*Damas approaches Deschappelles; converses apart with
> him in dumb show. Deschappelles shows him a paper,
> which he inspects, and takes.*

Pau. Thrice have I sought to speak; my courage fails me.
Sir, is it true that you have known—nay, are you
The friend of, Melnotte?

Mel.   Lady, yes! Myself
And Misery know the man!

Pau.   And you will see him,
And you will bear to him, ay, word for word,
All that this heart, which breaks in parting from him,
Would send, ere still for ever.

Mel.   He hath told me
You have the right to choose from out the world
A worthier bridegroom; he foregoes all claim,
Even to murmur at his doom. Speak on!

Pau. Tell him, for years I never nursed a thought
That was not his; that, on his wandering way,
Daily and nightly, pour'd a mourner's prayers.
Tell him ev'n now that I would rather share
His lowliest lot, walk by his side, an outcast, ·
Work for him, beg with him, live upon the light
Of one kind smile from him, than wear the crown

The Bourbon lost!

Mel.   [*Aside*] Am I already mad?
And does delirium utter such sweet words
Into a dreamer's ear? [*Aloud*] You love him thus,
And yet desert him?

Pau.   Say, that, if his eye
Could read this heart, its struggles, its temptations,
His love itself would pardon that desertion !
Look on that poor old man, he is my father ;
He stands upon the verge of an abyss !
He calls his child to save him ! Shall I shrink
From him who gave me birth? withhold my hand,
And see a parent perish ? Tell him this,
And say, that we shall meet again in heaven !

Mel. Lady—I—I—what is this riddle? what
The nature of this sacrifice?

Pau.   [*Pointing to Damas*] Go ask him !

Beau. [*From the table.*] The papers are prepared, we only need
Your hand and seal.

Mel.   Stay lady, one word more.
Were but your duty with your faith united,
Would you still share the low-born peasant's lot ?

Pau. Would I ? Ah, better death with him I love
Than all the pomp, which is but as the flowers
That crown the victim ! [*Turning away*] I am ready.

[*Melnotte rushes to Damas.*

Dam.   There,
This is the schedule, this the total.

Beau. [*To Deschappelles, showing notes*] These
Are yours the instant she has signed ; you are
Still the great House of Lyons !

[*The notary is about to hand the contract to Pauline, when
Melnotte seizes and tears it.*

Beau.   Are you mad ?

M. Des. How, sir ! What means this insult !

Mel.   Peace, old man !
I have a prior claim.   Before the face
Of man and heaven I urge it ; I outbid
Yon sordid huckster for your priceless jewel.

                                        [*Giving a pocket-book.*
There is the sum twice-told !   Blush not to take it :
There's not a coin that is not bought and hallow'd
In the cause of nations with a soldier's blood !
    Beau. Torments and death !
    Pau.   That voice !   Thou art—
    Mel.   Thy husband !
                                    [*Pauline rushes into his arms.*
    Mel. Look up ! Look up, Pauline ! for I can bear
Thine eyes !   The stain is blotted from my name.
I have redeemed mine honour.   I can call
On France to sanction thy divine forgiveness !   ·
Oh, joy !   Oh, rapture !   By the midnight watchfires
Thus have I seen thee ! thus foretold this hour !
And 'midst the roar of battle, thus have heard
The beating of thy heart against my own !
    Beau. Fool'd, duped, and triumph'd over in the hour
Of mine own victory !   Curses on ye both !
May thorns be planted in the marriage-bed !
And love grow sour'd and blacken'd into hate,
Such as the hate that gnaws me !
    Dam.   Curse away !
And let me tell thee, Beauseant, a wise proverb
The Arabs have : 'Curses are like young chickens,
[*Solemnly*] And still come home to roost !'
    Beau.   Their happiness
Maddens my soul !   I am powerless and revengeless.
                                            [*To Madame.*
I wish you joy !   Ha, ha ! the gardener's son !   [*Exit.*
    Dam. [*To Glavis*] Your friend intends to hang himself !
        Methinks

You ought to be his travelling companion !

Gla. Sir, you are exceedingly obliging !   [*Exit.*

Pau.   Oh !

My father, you are saved, and by my husband !

Ah ! blessed hour !

Mel.   Yet you weep still, Pauline !

Pau. But on thy breast ! *these* tears are sweet and holy !

M. Des. You have won love and honour, nobly, sir !

Take her ; be happy both !

Mme. D.   I'm all astonish'd !

Who, then, is Colonel Morier ?

Dam. ·   Y ou behold him !

Mel. Morier no more after this happy day !

I would not bear again my father's name

Till I could deem it spotless !   The hour's come !

Heaven smiled on conscience !   As the soldier rose

From rank to rank, how sacred was the fame

That cancell'd crime, and raised him nearer thee !

Mme. D. A colonel and a hero !   Well, that's something !

He's wond'rously improved !   I wish you joy, sir !

Mel. Ah ! the same love that tempts us into sin,

If it be true love, works out its redemption ;

And he who seeks repentance for the Past

Should woo the Angel Virtue in the future !   [*The curtain falls.*